ROTHERHAM LIBRARY & INFORMATION SERVICES

This book must be returned by the date specified at the time
of issue as the Date Due for Return.
The loan may be extended (personally, by post or telephone)
for a further period, if the book is not required by another
reader, by quoting the above number.

LM1(C)

For Fion

First published 1999 by Walker Books Ltd
87 Vauxhall Walk, London SE11 5HJ

2 4 6 8 10 9 7 5 3 1

© 1999 Vanessa Cabban

This book has been typeset in Horley Old Style.

Printed in Hong Kong

British Library Cataloguing in Publication Data
A catalogue record for this book is
available from the British Library.

ISBN 0-7445-6160-4 (hb)
ISBN 0-7445-6785-8 (pb)

Bertie and Small
and the Fast Bike Ride

Vanessa Cabban

WALKER BOOKS
AND SUBSIDIARIES
LONDON • BOSTON • SYDNEY

Today Bertie and Small
are playing outside.

Small is the rabbit
and Bertie wears the hat
with long floppy ears.

"Hold tight,"
says Bertie to Small.
"We're going around
the world."

Bertie is a fast driver.
Beep! Beep! Watch out!

Bertie rides over the desert.

Bump! Bump! Bump!

Bertie races through the grasslands.

Swish! Swish! Swish!

Bertie spins around the mountain.
Whoa!

Small almost falls out.

Bertie stops to help him.

At the edge of the forest,
Bertie looks for precious stones
and flowers for Mummy.

Then Bertie and Small
ride home. On the way
there's a rainstorm

but Bertie and Small don't mind.
They are on their way home
with treasure for Mummy.

"What brave travellers," says
Mummy. She loves the treasure.

And Mummy has something
for Bertie and Small.

A big welcome-home biscuit for Bertie.
A small welcome-home
biscuit for Small.

MORE WALKER PAPERBACKS
For You to Enjoy

BERTIE AND SMALL'S BRAVE SEA JOURNEY
by Vanessa Cabban

Another delightful book about Bertie and his soft-toy rabbit.
In this story they're setting out on a brave sea journey – in a box!

0-7445-6786-6   £3.99

TOM AND PIPPO
by Helen Oxenbury

There are six stories in each of these two colourful books
about toddler Tom and his special friend Pippo,
a soft-toy monkey.

"Just right for small children… A most welcome addition to
the nursery shelves." *Books for Keeps*

At Home with Tom and Pippo   0-7445-3721-5
Out and About with Tom and Pippo   0-7445-3720-7

£4.50 each